Mark and Michelle
in the mountains

MARCEL MARLIER

award publications

Mark and Michelle were spending their holidays in the mountains. One morning their parents said they might go for a walk along the path above the village.

"Perhaps we shall see some animals when we get right up there," Michelle said happily.

"I shouldn't think so—your red sweater will frighten them off." said Mark, who enjoyed teasing his sister.

They climbed higher and higher. And
suddenly a large bird, his neck
stretched and his tail fanned out
behind him, gave a loud cry.
"Gosh! That's a capercailzie,"
said Mark, who knew a lot about birds.
"He belongs to the grouse family and
his wife is called the greyhen."

"What are those then? Those over there? They look like birds of paradise," said Michelle.

"They're black cocks. They are calling because it's spring. Time for mating. Look at them quivering and shaking."

"They're going to attack each other!"

"Yes," said Mark. "Can you hear the hens in the long grass over there? They're cackling to cheer them on. When one of the cocks wins the hens will all flock to him."

Mark and Michelle crept quietly on round a bend in the path. They could see a mother rabbit and her three babies cleaning their fur.

"Those are mountain rabbits," whispered Mark. "In winter their fur is white so that they can't be seen against the snow. Then when the snow starts to melt they gradually grow darker."
Suddenly the mother rabbit pricked her ears up in alarm.

An enormous bird came swooping down on them. It was an eagle, and he was hungry. He had been soaring very high, hunting for food, when all at once he had spotted the rabbits far beneath him. Silently he dropped out of the sky, ready to seize his prey. Waving and shouting wildly, Mark and Michelle rushed towards him... the rabbits fled for their lives. Startled, the eagle gave up the chase and climbed upwards, with the wind, back to his mountain home.

Mark and Michelle scrambled up along the banks of the mountain stream until they reached a giant glacier lying in the hollow between two great peaks.

"Although the ice looks so solid, it's really moving all the time," said Michelle, who had read about this at school. "Inch by inch it's slowly sliding down towards the valley where it melts to form our stream." The children peered over the edge of a huge crevasse. "It's so deep I daren't look right down." said Michelle.

In the high valley beside the glacier they discovered a ptarmigan watching over her chicks.
"Don't move an inch, Michelle, they're very shy birds. They have three different plumages to camouflage themselves: white in winter, red in summer for the colour of the rocks, and white and brown stripes in the spring like the earth showing through the melting snow."

The mountain lake lay silent and still in its remote rocky basin.
Michelle took off her shoes and stockings to test the water. "It's
freezing," she said.

They could see the mountains
clearly reflected in its
motionless depths.
Four or five choughs were
riding on the air currents
overhead. The children
watched these small crows
spinning and diving, gliding
and somersaulting. What a
wonderful sight.

As they climbed away from the lake they heard a scatter of stones sliding off the side of the mountain, pattering against the rocks all the way down until they fell into the water below, sending ripples across its smooth surface.

The pebbles must have been dislodged by the herd of ibex they could see standing out against the sky.

The children watched them through Mark's binoculars. They knew that the females and kids stayed all day in the shelter of the rocks for safety—eagles are a particular threat, swooping down to seize a kid unless the mother can protect it with her own body. So it was the male ibexes they could see, standing guard on the rocky pinnacles. In spite of their size, some of them could leap considerable distances.

Mark adjusted his glasses to look further down the mountain. There, in the shade of a tree, he could see a mother chamois with a tiny kid. It was so unsteady on its legs that he guessed it

had only just been born. Its mother was ready to protect it from the dangers of the mountain during the first perilous hours of its life. Chamois are such timid creatures, rarely coming within human range, that Mark and Michelle were very fortunate to have spotted this pair.

Next they found
a family of marmots
that had made their home
on a grassy plateau at the top of a cliff.
The children saw that one of them was acting as sentry while the
others squatted on their haunches to nibble daintily at the grass
and tiny flowers.

Suddenly, the marmot on
watch gave the alarm and,
quick as a flash, all the
little creatures disappeared
into their burrow. Just in
time—it was the eagle again!
"Go away!" Michelle shouted.
Mark took off his sweater and
flapped it about.
The huge bird thwarted again, sailed away
to the mountain top.

"We are unfair to him," Mark said. "Up in his home his babies are probably crying with hunger."

"Why do birds and animals have to eat other animals?" demanded Michelle.

"That is what's unfair, if you ask me. Why can't animals all be vegetarians like elephants? They live on greenstuff.."

"Everything in
nature is part
of a pattern,"
explained Mark.
"Eagles usually snatch
sick or weak animals,
leaving the healthy
ones, and that helps to
control the spread of disease.
Vultures eat the flesh of dead animals, and leave the bones
to be cleared up by others. It seems cruel, maybe, but all the
pieces of the pattern fit together."

Now the sun was
sinking behind the
mountains, and Mark
and Michelle realised
they must set off
quickly if they were to
be home before dark.

On their way down they saw some crows mobbing an
eagle owl. They were flapping their wings at him and
cawing loudly to taunt him. But in a few hours, when

darkness fell, it would be his turn to go hunting — his small, round eyes would be able to pick out the slightest movement in the dark. "You see, there is no good or bad here," said Mark. "Every creature has to be on the look out, ready to kill... or be killed. It is the law of the wild."